I Am Invited to a Party!

To Cher and Trixie

ISBN 978-1-338-21370-6

12 11 10 9 8 7 6 5 4 3 2 1   17 18 19 20 21 22

Printed in the U.S.A.   40

First Scholastic printing, September 2017

I Am Invited to a Party!

An **ELEPHANT & PIGGIE** Book

By **Mo Willems**

SCHOLASTIC INC.

Gerald!

4

I am invited to a party!

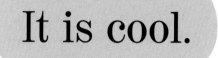

It is cool.

Will you go with me?

I have never been to a party.

I will go with you.

I *know* parties.

What if it is a fancy party?

16

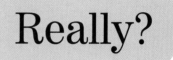

Really?

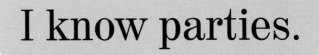

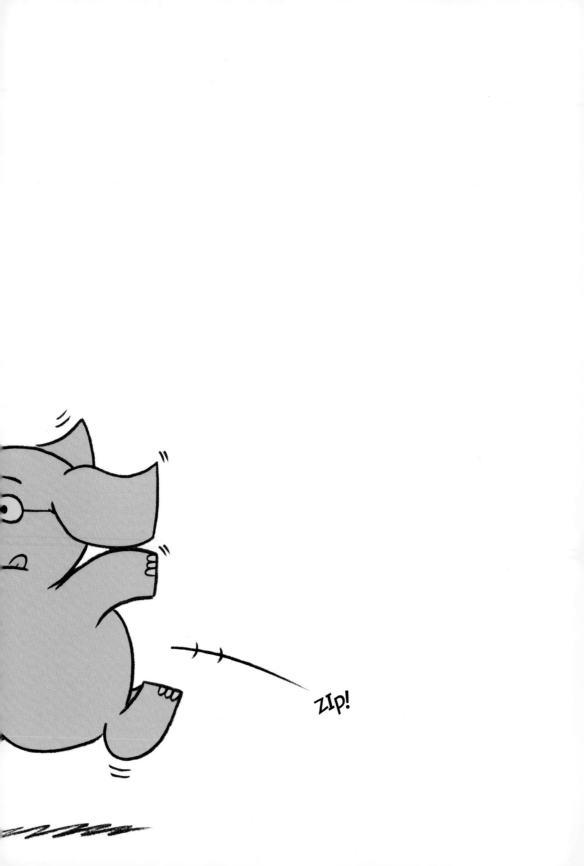

ZAp!

zip!

A fancy pool party?

He knows
parties.

zIp!

ZAP!

ZAP!

ZIp!

42

43

45

ZIP!

He had better
know parties. . . .

ZAp!

ZAP!

zip!

Well, that is a surprise.

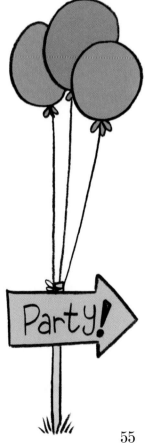

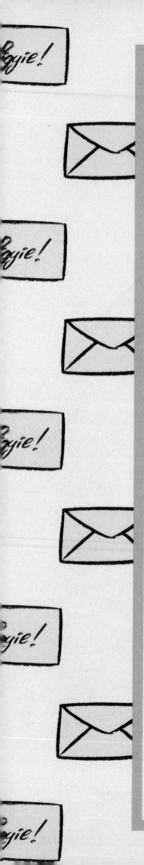

Have you read all of Elephant and Piggie's funny adventures?

Today I Will Fly!

My Friend Is Sad

I Am Invited to a Party!

There Is a Bird on Your Head!
(Theodor Seuss Geisel Medal)

I Love My New Toy!

I Will Surprise My Friend!

Are You Ready to Play Outside?
(Theodor Seuss Geisel Medal)

Watch Me Throw the Ball!

Elephants Cannot Dance!

Pigs Make Me Sneeze!

I Am Going!

Can I Play Too?

We Are in a Book!
(Theodor Seuss Geisel Honor)

I Broke My Trunk!
(Theodor Seuss Geisel Honor)

Should I Share My Ice Cream?

Happy Pig Day!

Listen to My Trumpet!

Let's Go for a Drive!
(Theodor Seuss Geisel Honor)

A Big Guy Took My Ball!
(Theodor Seuss Geisel Honor)

I'm a Frog!

My New Friend Is So Fun!

Waiting Is Not Easy!
(Theodor Seuss Geisel Honor)

I Will Take a Nap!

I *Really* Like Slop!

The Thank You Book